WALnootPOEDER
paardenbloem
lavendel kruid

WELCOME

When I was seven years old, my mother and I were feeding ducks alongside a river when a small wooden chest drifted by. My mother fished it out with a long tree branch. The chest was empty, but I knew just how to fill it.

During my childhood, I found small proofs of the existence of the supernatural. I accrued mystical, magical objects, and witnessed firsthand some of the creatures who left the objects behind. Most of the time the creatures were kind and harmless, but some were malicious, dangerous, and chilled me to the core.

As I grew older and began seeing the creatures as part of the natural order, my fear decreased. I'm still cautious in choosing where I swim, walk, and sleep, but I now know what to avoid. Every item in my small wooden chest is linked to a creature I have encountered in real life.

This book details my knowledge of monsters: the kind and the cruel. It answers questions like: How can you protect your houseplants, your hair, and your pets? And, what should you do if your compass suddenly stops working, or your pant legs are suddenly sewn shut? You can discover it all in *The Wonderful World of Eva*.

Copyright © 2022 Clavis Publishing Inc., New York

Originally published as *De wondere wereld van Eva* in Belgium and the Netherlands by Clavis Uitgeverij, 2021
English translation from the Dutch by Clavis Publishing Inc., New York

Visit us on the Web at www.clavis-publishing.com.

The Wonderful World of Eva written and illustrated by Eva Toorenent

ISBN 978-1-60537-737-7

This book was printed in February 2022 at Nikara,
M. R. Štefánika 858/25, 963 01 Krupina, Slovakia.

First Edition
10 9 8 7 6 5 4 3 2 1

Eva Toorenent

The Wonderful World of Eva

Clavis
NEW YORK

Personal Encounter:

While staying at my family's vacation home in France, I was building a cabin along the river with my brother, sister, and nieces. My niece and I decided that we needed more wood, so we walked upstream to look for materials. That's when I found a strange creature in the knee-deep water: a Diestrog. The creature looked distressed and used its claws to push a small pebble onto my foot. But it wasn't a normal pebble. It was an egg. I accepted the egg and promised to keep it safe. And it's a good thing I did. After doing some research, I discovered that if a Diestrog egg has no flower, the little one will die as soon as its egg hatches in daylight. I've kept it in my dark wooden chest ever since. I hope to one day find a way to make the egg hatch...

Species:
Troll

Subspecies:
Daylight Troll. Most trolls turn into stone when walking around during the day, but the daylight troll is a rare subspecies that thrives in sunlight.

Habitat:
Calm, clear rivers in France. They're also sometimes found in pools at the bottom of mountains.

Size:
The largest adult specimen is the size of a fat pumpkin. The smallest adult specimen is the size of an apple.

Food:
Small crabs and worms

Reproduction:
The reproduction process begins when a male releases its flower. This typically happens under a bridge, with ample protection from the sunlight. A female Diestrog catches the flower and eats it. She then lays eggs, from which new Diestrogs emerge several months later. Because of this strange reproductive process, Diestrogs are few in number.

Diestrog eggs appear like regular stones. A flower grows from the eggs before they hatch. Some of these flowers are picked by people. Picking a flower on a Diestrog egg isn't fatal to the little one or to the person who picks it, unless the egg hatches before a new flower has grown. Then the little one can't survive.

DIESTROG

If you pick a flower on an adult Diestrog during the day, both you and the Diestrog will turn to stone. If you pick the flower at night, you'll be cursed and never able to walk in daylight without turning to stone. The Diestrog will survive if it finds shelter and regrows its flower. This takes about a month. If it doesn't find shelter before the sun rises, it'll turn to stone and die.

The plants on a Diestrog's back vary according to their environment.

A Diestrog's flower resembles a water lily and only opens in sunlight.

The stone egg of a Diestrog is carried in a small hump under its flower.

Diestrogs are called Medusa stones in some villages because of their petrifying abilities.

Some people choose to keep Diestrogs as pets, but without adequate light, they'll gradually turn to stone.

Diestrog egg

A Diestrog wiggles its tail when it's happy.

Some creatures that can't survive in daylight, such as vampires, trolls, and certain witches, go out of their way to find Diestrogs at night and pick their flower. After all, the flower is very rare and has various magical properties. It's often used during rituals of dark witches. The Diestrog is then usually killed.

Diestrogs can walk, but very slowly. Their movements can be compared to those of a Stonefish.

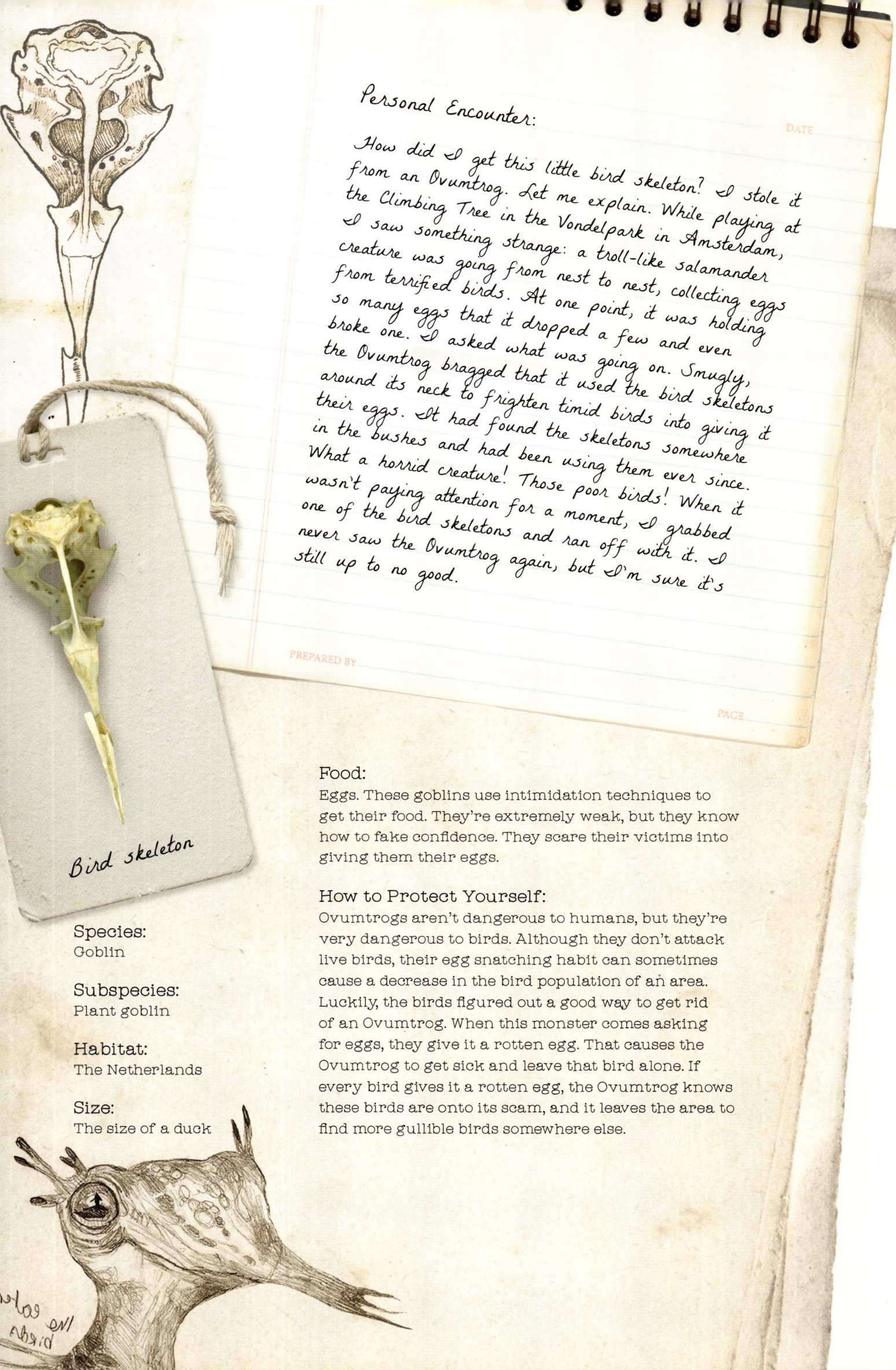

Personal Encounter:

How did I get this little bird skeleton? I stole it from an Ovumtrog. Let me explain. While playing at the Climbing Tree in the Vondelpark in Amsterdam, I saw something strange: a troll-like salamander creature was going from nest to nest, collecting eggs from terrified birds. At one point, it was holding so many eggs that it dropped a few and even broke one. I asked what was going on. Smugly, the Ovumtrog bragged that it used the bird skeletons around its neck to frighten timid birds into giving it their eggs. It had found the skeletons somewhere in the bushes and had been using them ever since. What a horrid creature! Those poor birds! When it wasn't paying attention for a moment, I grabbed one of the bird skeletons and ran off with it. I never saw the Ovumtrog again, but I'm sure it's still up to no good.

Bird skeleton

Species:
Goblin

Subspecies:
Plant goblin

Habitat:
The Netherlands

Size:
The size of a duck

Food:
Eggs. These goblins use intimidation techniques to get their food. They're extremely weak, but they know how to fake confidence. They scare their victims into giving them their eggs.

How to Protect Yourself:
Ovumtrogs aren't dangerous to humans, but they're very dangerous to birds. Although they don't attack live birds, their egg snatching habit can sometimes cause a decrease in the bird population of an area. Luckily, the birds figured out a good way to get rid of an Ovumtrog. When this monster comes asking for eggs, they give it a rotten egg. That causes the Ovumtrog to get sick and leave that bird alone. If every bird gives it a rotten egg, the Ovumtrog knows these birds are onto its scam, and it leaves the area to find more gullible birds somewhere else.

OVUMTROG

"Ovumtrog" is Latin for "egg troll," but these creatures aren't trolls. They're often confused with them.

Ovumtrogs are actually terrified of birds. But since eggs are their favorite food, they'll do anything to get some.

When bird eggs are scarce, this monster eats frog or fish eggs as a substitute.

This Ovumtrog is quite fat, which means it has been collecting eggs for a while.

An Ovumtrog's mouth is made to penetrate eggs without breaking them and to slurp out the insides.

This creature wears random bird skeletons around its neck to intimidate and scare birds. Some birds believe it and give it eggs to be left alone by this "bird killer."

Ovumtrogs are amphibians. They can breathe underwater and walk on the land.

Duck eggs are its favorite.

Personal Encounter:

When I was little, I found these gorgeous silver fairy earrings at a local market near my house. I begged my mother to buy them for me. Eventually, she gave in and I treasured my pretty jewelry. Not much later, my family and I went to Greece. During that trip, my little sister, Anna, wandered off. We eventually found her in the pool. She had almost drowned. After my stepmother pulled her out of the pool and made sure she was okay, I noticed something strange: a silver glint and a woolly ball-like creature rolled away from the scene. When we got back to our hotel room, I noticed that one of my earrings was missing. I knew it was no coincidence. I had been robbed by a Ball Bird!

DATE

Species:
Elf and realm walker. Although Ball Birds look and act a lot like birds, they're actually considered elves. They're known for their many thefts and other scummy behaviors. However, in addition to its talent for stealing all kinds of objects, the Ball Bird has a unique ability that not many creatures possess. It can roll back and forth between realms and does so at an incredible speed, which allows it to escape immediately after it has stolen something. That makes the Ball Bird not only an elf but also a realm walker.

Habitat:
Greece

Size:
About the size of a fat toad

Food:
This creature only eats stolen food. It doesn't matter if it's candy, a piece of meat, or a vegetable. As long as it's stolen, this creature will eat it.

How to Protect Yourself:
Don't wear shiny things, such as jewelry, coins, or sparkly outfits. While this creature may not seem dangerous, it is. Ball Birds are excellent thieves and love to create elaborate distractions to make their heist more successful. These distractions are usually harmless, but they can lead to life-threatening situations, like the incident with my sister, for example. Who knows what would have happened to her if we hadn't gotten there in time . . .

Reproduction:
Male Ball Birds attract females with shiny things. The larger their collection, the greater their chances of finding a mate. But these animals are also known to steal among themselves. If a male has a bigger and better collection of shiny things, other Ball Birds will notice and start stealing from him. Therefore, it's no coincidence that the nests of Ball Birds are always quite close to one another. If you see a nest with shiny things, you can almost be sure that it belongs to a Ball Bird.

BALL BIRD

A Ball Bird has wings, but it can't fly with them. It can, however, use them to protect its head while rolling.

Ball Birds are considered half-mad because they live in several worlds at once, but they aren't fully present in any of them.

This bird-like creature can't fly, but it can roll. Of course, that isn't a super-fast way to escape unless it's on a hill. That's why a Ball Bird rolls back and forth between realms. It steals something in the human world and then rolls back to the spirit realm. It also uses this ability to go to places it wouldn't normally be able to go. That way, it can build a nest high in a tree.

Magpies and crows have a reputation for stealing shiny things, but that's Ball Bird trickery. It's likely that people who found nests of Ball Birds mistakenly assumed they were nests of magpies or crows. After all, Ball Birds are excellent framers. For centuries, these crafty con artists have been making sure that magpies and crows are falsely accused of stealing shiny objects.

Fairy earring

Personal Encounter:

When I was a little kid, I had long, blond hair that reached my hips. Although my hair was very pretty, it also required a lot of brushing, combing, and grooming. I hated that. One day, I wore a tight ponytail and went for a walk in the forest with my parents. Suddenly, out of the corner of my eye, I saw a creature that looked like a little woman. She was sitting on top of a rabbit. Before I knew it, she had tried to cut my hair off with her teeth. Fortunately, my father also saw what was happening. He picked me up, and we left the forest immediately. Later, I told the strange story to my grandmother. She silently opened a box containing two long, brown braids. It contained a small note that read: braids Jeanne, age 13, 1947. My grandmother told me that the same thing had happened to her when she was thirteen years old and that she was actually relieved when it happened. She hated her long hair tremendously, but her mother didn't allow her to cut it off. I think the Wild Women sensed that my grandmother and I weren't happy with our long hair, and they wanted to help us.

Grandma Jeanne

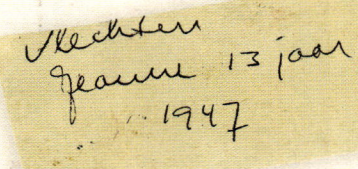

Vlechten
Jeanne 13 jaar
1947

How to Protect Yourself:

Wild Women usually target children because they often have no control over what happens to their hair. In addition, they sometimes try to help adults who dislike their long hair, for example, when their partner doesn't want them to get their hair cut. If you want to keep your hair safe, I recommend that you always wear your hair the way you like it!

Reproduction:

Like other fairies, Wild Women are born from primordial trees, but those are becoming increasingly scarce. As a result, no new Wild Women have been seen for a long time. However, as long as a Wild Woman has hair, she can live an exceptionally long life. It's possible that the Wild Woman who helped my grandmother may have been the same one who tried to cut off my hair.

Species:
Fairy

Habitat:
Forests in the Netherlands, Belgium, and France

Size:
The size of a small rabbit, but they're a tiny bit lighter. This allows them to ride rabbits.

Food:
Berries, mushrooms, and insects. If a Wild Woman is starving, she sometimes eats mice and small birds as well.

WILD WOMAN

Most of the time, these creatures leave people alone, but if they see a child who isn't happy with their long hair, they'll sneak up and cut off the hair with their teeth. They want to free children who feel trapped by the fuss of braids and ponytails.

Wild Women never cut, braid, or comb their hair. It contains their strength, so they'll protect it at all costs. It's said that if you brush the hair of a Wild Woman, you'll lose your own hair forever.

If you cut a Wild Woman's hair, she'll die.

They ride wild rabbits. Therefore, these rabbits are at ease with humanoid creatures. If you see a wild rabbit that's a little too comfortable around people, it's undoubtedly the rabbit of a Wild Woman.

Wild Women find it very disturbing that some people have no hair. They're surprised that bald people can walk and aren't dead!

Herb collection in pillbox {

Walnootpoeder
paardenbloem
zaad
laverdel kruid

DATE

Personal Encounter:

When I was young, I found an old book at a flea market: The Great Herbal Pharmacy by Lex Overeijnder. In that book, there was the following curious fact: if you wear a necklace of ground ivy from April 30 to May 1, you can see witches. Of course, I wanted to know if this was really true. After hours of collecting ground ivy, my necklace was finally finished. I wore it on the evening of April 30. That's when I saw the Maledalis, a funny creature that loves to cuddle, play, and collect different kinds of herbs. It appeared out of thin air in the middle of my room and asked me if I wanted to go with it to a safe place, the April 31 realm, to hide from people who burned witches. I politely declined and said that hadn't happened here for hundreds of years. The Maledalis looked pleasantly surprised, smiled at me, and disappeared. After our encounter, I started my own herb collection and did some more research on the April 31 realm. What I found was astounding...

Species:
Realm walker. A realm walker is a being that can travel to different worlds. In fact, Maledalises are so powerful that they can take others with them. They can even open and create new realms.

Habitat:
This creature only lives in our world on Walpurgis Night. That's the night of April 30 to May 1. It's when witches are burned all over Europe. It's also when witches are most powerful and easiest to find. Witch hunters use this to their advantage. Maledalises help witches on Walpurgis Night by transporting them to the April 31 realm, a secret day between April 30 and May 1. In that realm, witches can relax, converse, and practice magic in a safe place. When May 1 ends, the witches return to Europe.

Size:
The size of a small monkey and extremely lightweight

Food:
Flowers. Sometimes they accidentally eat their own tail. Don't worry, it grows back.

How to Protect Yourself:
Maledalises are extremely friendly, but they might eat all the flowers in your garden. To avoid this, burn a witch in your garden, preferably on Walpurgis Night. You'll curse your garden for decades, and the Maledalises will not likely return. After all, they're considered allies of witches. If you attack one of their friends, they'll avoid your house like the plague. However, they might linger around your property to warn other witches.

How to Attract this Creature:
If you want to see this creature and visit the secret April 31 realm, pretend to be a witch and wear a necklace of ground ivy on April 30. If a Maledalis suspects that you're in danger of being burned on Walpurgis Night, it'll offer you an escape to the other realm.

MALEDALIS

The large number of witches burned on Walpurgis Night didn't go unnoticed in other realms. The Maledalis saw that they were losing their friends at an alarming rate. They decided this wasn't acceptable and created a secret realm: the April 31 realm. There, witches are safe.

Its coat is covered with growing ground ivy. A beautiful purple flower also hangs from the end of its tail.

The Maledalis helps anyone who needs to flee from witch hunts on the night of April 30 to May 1. Therefore, it's called the protector of all witches.

Because of the Maledalises, there were no witches left to burn on April 30. That's why villagers and townspeople burned fake witches made of wood and hay. In the Czech Republic, they still observe this practice on Pálení čarodějnic.

HARPIES

In villages that allow a controlled Harpy population, the people who live there aren't the friendliest. They're willing to give up certain freedoms to prevent outsiders from visiting their village. They overfeed their children so they can't easily be kidnapped, and they live in constant fear of being picked off and killed by a Harpy.

People living in "Harpy-friendly" villages almost all have severe back pain. As children, they have to wear heavy weights on their belts and backs when they're outside to make them too heavy for Harpies to carry. They can go without weights once they're adults, but usually the damage has been done by then.

Some male Harpies that are too small to join a harem try a trick. They eat a baby Harpy when the parents aren't looking and take the baby's place. But a young Harpy that isn't growing is suspicious. When the other young grow larger than the imposter, the parents will get suspicious and kill the phony child.

Species:
Harpy. There are several subspecies around the world. The smallest live in Europe and the largest in Africa.

Habitat:
Mountainous areas in Europe, North America, Africa, and Asia. Villages near mountains sometimes allow a "controlled" Harpy population because an active Harpy nest scares away bandits. Villagers often feed the Harpies a small portion of their livestock to keep them happy.

Size:
Some males are the size of a crow, and others are closer to the size of a pony. Females are usually a lot bigger. The largest female Harpy ever recorded was near Mount Kilimanjaro in Tanzania. She was about the size of an elephant.

Food:
Primarily cattle, but there are many accounts of children and even small adults being carried away by these fearsome creatures. Cannibalism is also not uncommon among Harpies. If there isn't enough food for the young, a male Harpy is sometimes sacrificed to feed them. Thus, the males must always provide enough food. Otherwise, they themselves become the supper.

How to Protect Yourself:
You can recognize the territory of a Harpy by the village that's part of it. Most residents are particularly unfriendly. If you ask them for directions, they ignore you. Almost all the children are heavyset, and they never walk the streets alone. If they do, they wear weighted belts and backpacks. In addition, there are often spikes on the houses, and sheep and goats surround the village. Run like the wind if you come across such a village.

Reproduction:
Male Harpies are a lot weaker and smaller than females. Because of her size, the female needs a lot of food while laying eggs. Therefore, she usually has a harem of about three to seven males to fetch her food. The larger the female, the larger the harem.

Blue feather

Personal Encounter:

When I was twelve years old, I went on a trip to the Swiss Alps with my family. As we drove through the valley, it started to get dark. My father decided to find a place to spend the night. Fortunately, there was a village with a small inn at the bottom of the mountain. As my family entered the building, I saw two large red eyes glowing in the darkness across the street. Bewildered, I continued to stare at them until I was alone. Suddenly, the murderous creature with red eyes seized its opportunity. It came flying at me at full speed. Just before it could swoop me away, my father stepped outside to see what was keeping me. The creature saw him, stopped its attack, and flew away screeching. A small feather swirled on the ground. I put it in my pocket. The next day we left in a hurry. I'm not sure if my father saw the monster, but after that, he always carefully researched where we would stay during our travels.

Personal Encounter:

DATE

My family and I went to Pompeii a few years ago. As I walked through the streets of the forgotten city, looking at the ancient buildings and the plaster casts of bodies, I saw something bright red emerging from behind a large rock. My family walked on, but I went to investigate. The red thing turned out to be some kind of dragon. A Dragosaur, I later discovered. The monster slowly approached me. I was startled, but when I saw its friendly gaze, I calmed down a bit. As the Dragosaur came closer, I saw that it had something in its mouth. Suddenly, it dropped the object, turned around, and disappeared into the forest. On the ground was a small, brown stone. Of course, I couldn't refuse the gracious gift and took the little stone to add to my collection of curious things.

Species:
Dragosaur. Although a Dragosaur is similar to a full-blooded dragon, it isn't a real dragon. Sir Richard Owen, the creator of the term "dinosaur," considered Dragosaurs to be the link between dinosaurs and dragons. It's a scientific miracle that these creatures still exist. They're like the city of Pompeii: frozen in time.

Habitat:
The volcano Vesuvius in Pompeii, Italy

Size:
About the size of an average six-year-old child (almost four feet)

Food:
Birds, deer, and small rodents

How to Protect Yourself:
Dragosaurs feel responsible for the eruption of Mount Vesuvius in 79 AD. The sense of guilt has been passed down from generation to generation to ensure that they never make the same mistake again. That's why these creatures are so friendly to humans. However, they're dangerous to dogs and cats.

Reproduction:
Dragosaurs lay their eggs in the middle of Mount Vesuvius. They can tolerate incredible heat, but they aren't entirely fireproof. If you put a Dragosaur in magma or lava, it'll most certainly burn.

Stone from Pompeii

DRAGOSAUR

When humans first settled in Pompeii, Dragosaurs had been living there for thousands of years. They were anything but happy with the new inhabitants, but they eventually came around thanks to great efforts made by the humans. They regarded the Dragosaurs as sacred creatures and treated them with respect and dignity. That way, both species learned to live together in harmony.

The people of Pompeii even gave the Dragosaurs gifts to placate them. Usually, these were pretty stones. The Dragosaurs kept all the gifts they received in Mount Vesuvius. Over time, however, the collection of stones began to grow dangerously large. The collected layer of hard stone increased the pressure inside the volcano exponentially. That eventually led to the eruption of Mount Vesuvius in 79 AD. Thousands of people lost their lives back then. The Dragosaurs still feel guilty for causing the deaths of so many people. To make up for their horrible mistake, Dragosaurs now give stones to humans instead of the other way around.

Thousands of people died, but after the disaster, it was recorded that many bodies had disappeared without a trace. What had happened to all those corpses? Well, there's a possible explanation. When Dragosaurs lose one of their loved ones, they cremate the body by throwing it into the magma of Mt. Vesuvius. It's believed that these creatures cremated many of the victims at the center of the volcano.

The second reason Dragosaurs give stones to humans is to ensure that history doesn't repeat itself. If there are fewer stones in Pompeii, there's a smaller chance that Vesuvius will erupt again. Personally, I don't know if that will help, but I understand the thought process.

GRASS DRAGON

Just one drop of dragon's blood can raise the dead. But be warned: it might happen differently than you expect.

Dragons are very difficult to kill because of their crazy life-giving blood. So crazy in fact that if a dragon loses blood, it can be restored. Sometimes other things will crawl into the dragon's body, such as sand, stones, and sticks, and it'll fuse with them. That's why there are so many types of dragons, such as Mushroom Dragons, Volcanic Dragons, and Earth Dragons.

Dogs are incredibly frightened of the Grass Dragon's bell. This fear has spread beyond the borders of the United Kingdom. My dog Baloe, who was bred and raised in the Netherlands, is terrified of the sound of the bell.

The Grass Dragon is extremely good at camouflaging. It also sleeps a lot. It's possible that you've encountered a grass dragon without even realizing it.

Personal Encounter:

I met this creature when I was visiting a friend in Oxford. While waiting for her to finish her classes, I decided to take a walk in the countryside of Uffington. In the grassy fields, I found something peculiar: a gold bell on a string, lying in the grass. When I picked up the bell, the string to which it was attached snapped. Suddenly, a dragon covered in grass emerged from the ground. Before I understood what was happening, the beast had already run away happily. When I returned home and showed the bell to my family, one of my dogs began shaking uncontrollably. He ran up the stairs and hid in a corner. After some research, I realized that I had probably encountered the Grass Dragon.

Baloe

Bell

Species:
Dragon

Habitat:
The United Kingdom. Although its home territory is Uffington, Oxfordshire, the Grass Dragon has vacationed in Ireland and other English locations. It's easy to find: look for areas with a decrease in dog population.

Size:
As tall as a human and as long as an anaconda

Food:
The Grass Dragon is a monster with two natures: grass and dragon. The grass part of this creature likes fertilizer, good soil, and sunlight. But the dragon part likes a good piece of (dog) meat once in a while.

How to Protect Yourself:
Luckily for us, the Grass Dragon doesn't attack humans unless provoked. But it absolutely hates dogs. After all, they pee on grass, pee is rich in nitrogen, and nitrogen is known to kill grass. Moreover, dogs love to dig and play, often destroying the grass while doing so. To protect its precious blades, the Grass Dragon kills all dogs it encounters. A few frustrated farmers reacted by giving the dragon a necklace with a bell designed to warn any nearby dogs of the dragon's presence. In hindsight, I shouldn't have taken the bell with me . . .

Transformation:
At first, the Grass Dragon was a normal dragon. It ate people, spat fire, terrorized villages . . . Until the day St. George came along to defeat him. Or so he thought. Most people don't realize that the monster hadn't died, but was mortally wounded. It lost nearly all of its blood. As the dragon lay dying and its blood gushed onto the grass, the blades began to grow faster and faster. The hungry grass craved more dragon blood. It even began to crawl up and enter the dragon's body through the open wounds. During that process, the grass fused with the dragon. Although that sounds gruesome, it actually saved its life. The fusion changed the dragon's nature and its appearance. Its diet also became different: the dragon was no longer interested in devouring humans, but in eating fertilizer and drinking lots of water. Its modified nature also gave this monster a new archenemy, namely dogs.

Personal Encounter:

When I moved into my new house this year, something strange happened to my plants. They all died. I had no idea why this was happening, until one day I saw the culprit: Mr. Rottingham, a grumpy, slimy little plant goblin who appeared screaming out of the earth around one of my dead plants. He shouted at the top of his lungs that he would mercifully kill all my "imprisoned" plants. Of the various methods I tried to get rid of him, one finally worked: getting rid of all my plants. I thought that would be the end of it. Then my mother-in-law gave me a new plant for my birthday. It lived for one hour...

Dead plant: the work of Mr. Rottingham

Species:
Goblin

Habitat:
Houses, flower stores, and garden centers in Western Europe

Size:
About the size of a plump pear

Food:
Sunlight, water, and manure. Lots and lots of manure.

Objective:
Mr. Rottingham gets furious when he sees houseplants. He thinks plants belong in the wild, not indoors. Therefore, he "saves" houseplants by killing them out of mercy. He hopes to convince people that they're bad at taking care of plants and thus discourage them from buying new ones. If all your houseplants die without reasonable cause, this creature might be to blame.

How to Protect Yourself:
If you buy a plant or receive one as a gift, always check it very closely. Mr. Rottingham is often lurking about, waiting for the right moment to hitchhike a houseplant. If he does invade your home, it's very difficult to get rid of him. You'll need to get rid of all your plants as soon as possible. Plastic plants are a safe alternative, but Mr. Rottingham has been spotted several times trying to kill those as well.

Withered leaf of a chestnut tree

MR. ROTTINGHAM

Mr. Rottingham would rather see plants die than watch them be held "hostage". He's a plant activist.

He likes to stick his long nose into the business of others.

His rotting arms are sometimes harvested by witches. Just a small piece can corrupt farmland and crops for decades to come.

He's not very smart, but he's very aggressive.

Mr. Rottingham has rotting root hands. Everything he touches rots.

His rot contaminates not only plants, but also other things, such as relationships, ideas, and projects. That's why it's important to get rid of him as soon as possible.

Personal Encounter:

I have fortunately never met a Boletustrog, but my great-grandmother has. She was visiting the grave of a loved one when she suddenly saw a hand wiggling itself out of the ground. She cautiously went closer to inspect the hand. Suddenly, a huge troll emerged from the ground. The monster wanted to attack her, but it hesitated when it saw that she was wearing a gold earring. Out of fear, my great-grandmother began to convulse, causing the jewel to fall to the ground. The troll saw the earring lying there, took its chance, and ate the poor woman in one bite. However, it hadn't considered that earrings come in pairs. As soon as the gold of the other earring touched its tongue, the Boletustrog felt a burning sensation and spit out the poor woman. She fortunately didn't sustain any injuries. I inherited the earrings and will never visit a cemetery without them.

Species:
Troll

Subspecies:
Mushroom troll

Habitat:
Graveyards, old burial grounds, and catacombs in the United Kingdom and the Netherlands. Boletustrogs prefer rainy climates. It's believed that centuries ago, they also lived in India, but in time grew extinct.

Size:
Quite large. Their upper body is about the length and width of a tall obese man. The length of the lower body is unknown.

Food:
Humans. They especially prefer the lean, tasty meat of children.

How to Protect Yourself:
Gold is the only known method of repelling this type of troll. In many cultures, it's considered a symbol of the sun and enlightenment: everything this creature hates. In India, it's customary to put a piece of gold in the mouth of a deceased person. It'll protect the body from the Boletustrog. If a Boletustrog does appear in a graveyard, avoid the location for two days. The Boletustrog will disappear on its own, leaving a black foaming substance behind. Wear something made of gold when you return to the graveyard and keep an eye out for dead man's fingers. These mushrooms indicate the presence of a Boletustrog. If you see such a mushroom, leave the graveyard immediately.

Reproduction:
Boletustrogs are hermaphrodites and can multiply on their own. But when they do, they immediately die themselves. This explains why there aren't many Boletustrogs.

Gold earrings

BOLETUSTROG

The mushrooms this troll regurgitates are called dead man's fingers, because they resemble the hands of dead people. The troll uses this feature to its advantage. It hides in the ground near a fresh grave. When people come to mourn the deceased, the Boletustrog slowly wiggles its mushrooms. The visitors then think the deceased is still alive and try to help them. When they grab the mushrooms, the troll emerges from the earth to devour them.

These creatures are highly allergic to sunlight, but they can endure it in small amounts. If the sky is overcast, they can temporarily appear above the ground during the day.

Sometimes a Boletustrog will appear above the ground and try to lure someone by convincing them that they can talk to the dead. The troll tells them what their loved one was wearing when they were buried. It knows this because it opened the grave beforehand. Once the victim draws near, the Boletustrog strikes and devours them.

Boletustrogs are bound to the place where they emerge from the ground, so they can't chase you. They can move around, but it takes a lot of effort and time.

If Boletustrogs are exposed to direct sunlight, they immediately turn to stone. Fortunately, they can't cause many casualties because most cemeteries have a curfew that begins at sunset and ends at sunrise.

1801-1997
R.I.P
✝
WITCH

1681
UNKNOWN

Personal Encounter:

Have you ever had a sudden inexplicable urge to jump off a tall building or leap in front of a subway even though you had no desire to die? Well, the French have a word for that: "l'appel du vide." That means the call of the void. This strange impulse is caused by the Voidolf, a terrifying monster that has probably tried to push you off buildings or in front of traffic hundreds of times. But it isn't psychologically strong enough to make you do it. That's why you only get the eerie feeling of wanting to jump or run into traffic. You have to be careful, though, because this creature can grow more powerful and throw you off balance.

Fortunately, my own encounter with a Voidolf wasn't dangerous. When I was about six years old, I found this beautiful stone in my grandparents' garden. I took it upstairs to play with it. Hanging out of the window with the stone in my hand, I felt a sudden impulse to drop it. And I did. Then I spent the entire day looking for it in the garden. While searching for my pretty stone, I saw a strange blue monster out of the corner of my eye. It looked at me and grinned. When I found the stone, the creature suddenly disappeared. Since then, I've been keeping the stone in my small wooden chest, hoping it'll somehow protect me from Voidolfs.

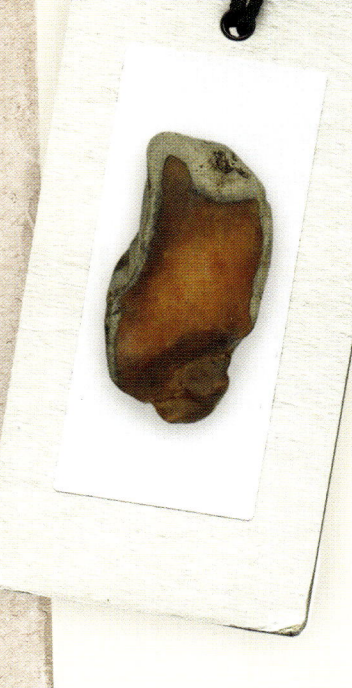

Call of the
void stone

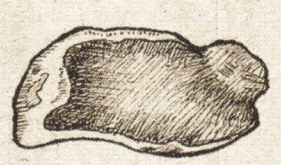

Species:
Spirit

Habitat:
Places with immediate potential for danger, such as bridges, tall buildings, and train stations.

Size:
The size of a human's upper body. Voidolfs don't have legs and don't need any.

Food:
Negative energy. For example, if you drop your phone in the river, you feel sad. The feeling you radiate makes a tasty snack for a Voidolf.

How to Protect Yourself:
If a Voidolf wants you to jump, run, or drop something, don't do it. Giving in to this spirit will make it stronger and bolder, and other people might get hurt. If you've dropped something, find it again as soon as possible. Voidolfs haven't killed many people yet, but you definitely don't want to encourage them.

How to Attract This Creature:
Standing in a dangerous place is the best way to attract a Voidolf. You probably won't see it, because it's usually invisible. However, it becomes visible if you do what it wants you to do.

VOIDOLF

These creatures are only fully visible if you carry out what they want you to do. Voidolfs aren't very powerful, though, so fortunately, not many people have spotted one yet.

Voidolfs can't make people act on impulse, but they try to. And they do reinforce the feeling of despair in certain places.

The Voidolf is typically a solitary creature, but clusters of these spirits can be found on the Golden Gate Bridge and in other places where people might wander when they're feeling very, very sad. The Voidolfs feed on the strong negative energy that lingers there.

Voidolfs are one of the weakest types of spirits. They can only evoke fleeting feelings.

Personal Encounter:

A while ago, my grandmother passed away. She didn't understand our goodbyes to her because she was suffering from dementia. A few days after she died, my grandfather was practicing his funeral speech out loud. He was home alone, but when he uttered the final sentence of the speech – "Goodbye, Loekie, we'll miss you – a glass teapot suddenly broke in the kitchen. My grandfather believes it was my grandmother's way of saying goodbye one last time. After all, many people believe that the spirits of the dead will break glass or porcelain to say goodbye to their loved ones. But for some spirits, it can be difficult to make contact with the physical world. Fortunately, there's a creature that's happy to help those spirits: the Shard Demon.

Glass shard

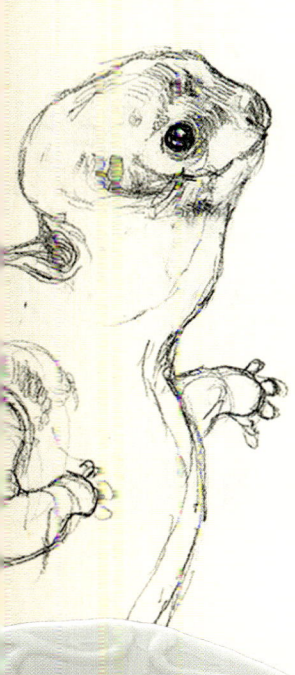

Species:
Demon. Shard demons are also called the messengers of the dead. Since they're demons, they can manipulate the physical world much better than human spirits. Therefore, spirits often ask them to help communicate with living relatives.

Habitat:
Where things need to be broken and restless spirits can be found, this ghostly creature will appear. When Shard Demons aren't causing mayhem by breaking things, they hang out at the border between the land of the dead and the land of the living.

Size:
The size of a teacup

Food:
Glass and porcelain. When a Shard Demon breaks things for ghosts, it always eats a few shards. That's its reward.

How to Protect Yourself:
The name "Shard Demon" may sound scary, but there's nothing to be afraid of. When a Shard Demon visits you, it's usually because a loved one wants to see you one last time. So, you have nothing to fear if one of your family members has recently died and a random object breaks in your house. But you shouldn't walk around barefoot then. You might accidentally step on a piece of glass.

How to Attract This Creature:
A Shard demon needs a reason to travel to your house. If you don't have a loved one who has passed away, it's almost impossible to get a visit from a Shard Demon. But if you know someone who has recently died, you want to make it as easy as possible for that person to say goodbye to you. Therefore, put lots of bottles, glasses, teapots, and so on near the edges of tables. That way, it's easier for the Shard Demon to shatter something.

SHARD DEMON

Shard Demons are usually summoned by spirits who were unable to say goodbye to their friends and family when they were alive.

Its horns indicate its demonic origin, but it isn't an evil demon: just a simple guy living on the border between two worlds with a love of breaking things.

Every time a Shard Demon breaks something, a new crack appears on its skin.

This creature's skin has the same texture as broken glass and porcelain, but it isn't solid. Its body is translucent and quite flexible, allowing the Shard Demon to disappear within seconds.

Most spirits will ask a Shard Demon to smash something for them. Why do spirits want something made of glass or porcelain to break? It's because broken glass and porcelain are mirrors to the other side. If one of their loved ones looks into a shard of glass or porcelain, the spirits living on the other side can see them one last time.

A Shard Demon is a speedy little fellow. If it pays you a visit, you probably won't even notice. But there's a way you can tell if one has come by. As soon as you try to fix a broken object, you'll notice that a few shards are missing. That's because the Shard Demon always eats a few shards. If you can't reconstruct a broken object because pieces are missing, a Shard Demon has probably been involved.

Personal Encounter:

When I was seventeen years old, I went to Paris with my mother to explore the catacombs under the city. Because we arrived very late and were the last people allowed into the catacombs that day, my mother and I were able to walk through the catacombs all by ourselves for an hour. Or so we thought... In a deep dark corridor, I saw something coming towards us. Something big. The monster didn't seem to notice us. It looked like a walking skeleton covered in an almost translucent layer of loose skin, and it casually stacked skulls on top of each other. I gasped. In slow motion, the creature looked at me. It startled when it saw me, then turned around and wobbled away. I picked up a pebble from the ground that the creature had dropped during its flight. That was the first and only time I encountered a Bone Stacker.

Stone from the catacombs in Paris

Species:
Scavenger

Habitat:
Graveyards, old burial grounds, and catacombs. Sometimes they can even be seen on battlefields.

Size:
On average about eight feet tall, but they can even grow ten to thirteen feet tall. How does such a large creature move around in the catacombs, you might ask? Its body and bones are incredibly soft. It fits into almost anything, and it always bounces back to its normal proportions.

Food:
Corpses. Bone Stackers are scavengers. They don't touch living beings.

How to Protect Yourself:
Bone Stackers are attracted to anything dead, but they do have a preference for deceased humans. If you're near someone who dies in the territory of a Bone Stacker, he'll be there within minutes. An encounter can be frightening, but it never has a fatal outcome. After all, Bone Stackers are terribly afraid of living things and will do everything they can to avoid coming into contact with "creepy" warm bodies. The best thing you can do in the presence of a Bone Stacker is to stay alive.

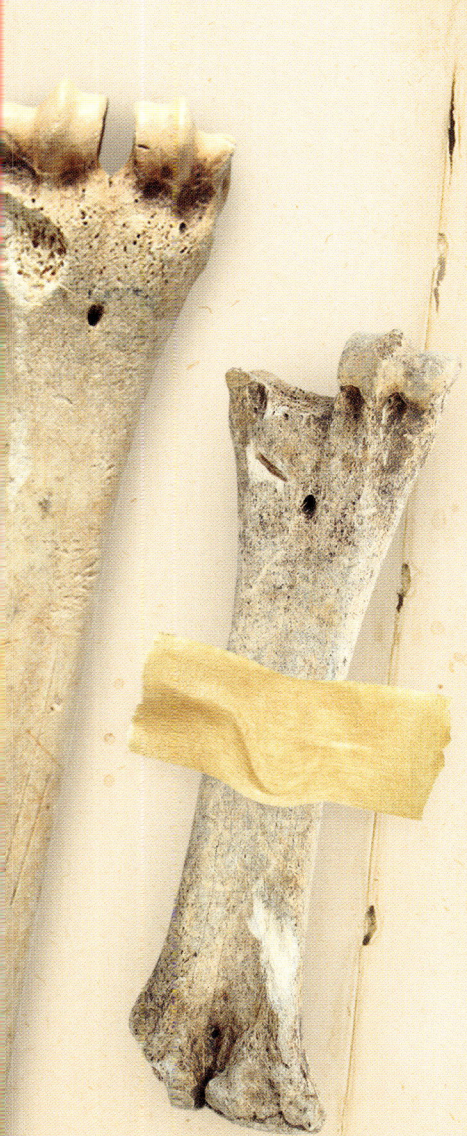

BONE STACKER

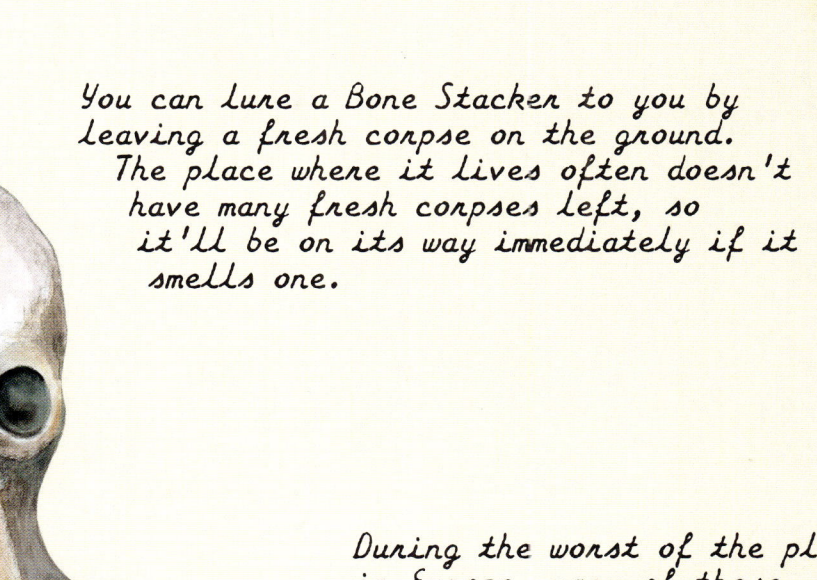

You can lure a Bone Stacker to you by leaving a fresh corpse on the ground. The place where it lives often doesn't have many fresh corpses left, so it'll be on its way immediately if it smells one.

Their hands have evolved to hold skulls more efficiently. The two long fingers go into the eye sockets, and the smaller finger in the middle goes into the nasal cavity.

During the worst of the plagues in Europe, many of these monsters were captured. They were fed corpses of people who had died of the plague. That way, there were fewer corpses to spread the disease. This fact isn't widely known because it was part of a government cover-up.

Bone Stackers are very artistic creatures. They consider stacking bones an art form. The work in the Sedlec Ossuary in the Czech Republic was created by what must have been the Michelangelo of Bone Stackers. That creature was truly a master of the craft!

Unfortunately, Bone Stackers have a bad reputation. People associate them with death, which is understandable. But without them, the plague would have been a lot harder to fight. Bone stackers and other scavengers are vital to stopping the spread of diseases and the horrible smell of dead people.

They use the skin flaps on their bodies to clean and polish bones.

Here you see
the Jelly Fox.

I discovered it
in Egypt when I was
eleven years old.
That encounter made
quite an impression on
me. After all, the Jelly
Fox stands out from the other
creatures in this book. It's the
creature that sparked my love for
all things strange and unexplainable,
and we've been connected ever since.
It has reappeared in my life a few
times, especially during life-changing
experiences. Those experiences weren't
always positive, but they did eventually
change my life for the better. I often
try to draw or paint the Jelly Fox
when I see it. It evolves and changes
with the times, just like me. I know
very little about this species, but I
consider it my guardian angel. That's
why I had to include it in this book.

I filled this bottle with murky water
from a lake when I was at a creative
low. The Jelly Fox appeared floating
above the water, and I saw that it
was slowly deteriorating, just like the
murky lake water that was once so clear.
That made me realize I needed to get out of
a murky situation I was in. I keep the bottle
as a reminder to never let myself get into a
situation like that again.

Swamp water

Ribben
bystostler

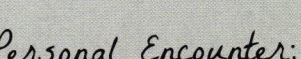

Personal Encounter:

Long ago, the village of Breskens in the Netherlands almost fell victim to a horrible Tridentum trend. My grandmother lived there. When she was about six years old, all the children of the village had to have their tonsils removed. They had to wait in a long line at the doctor's office. Within a few hours, no child in Breskens had any tonsils left. But why, you ask? Well, when a village suddenly decides to remove wisdom teeth, tonsils, hair, appendixes, and other "useless" human bits, it's usually because a Tridentum has visited, and they don't want a trend to start. A Tridentum is a creature that likes to collect human body parts to wear as accessories. Although I've never seen a Tridentum before, I believe I had to have my wisdom teeth removed because of this creature.

Species:
Elf

Subspecies:
Water elf

Habitat:
Waters in Western Europe

Size:
The size of a long, slender man

Food:
Only the best and rarest berries. Strangely, these creatures are vegan.

How to Protect Yourself:
If you see a Tridentum during the day, you're perfectly safe. That's when it wants to be seen, as it loves it when people look at them. However, it's almost impossible to bump into a Tridentum at night. If it doesn't want to be seen, you won't see it. If you somehow come across a Tridentum during the night, try to stay as calm as possible. If you're lucky, it'll pass you. But if you're unlucky and it chooses to collect something from you, just let it happen. It'll only harvest body parts that you don't really need, such as wisdom teeth, tonsils, appendixes, hair, nails, and so on.

You may want to take the precaution of having body parts removed that Tridenta are known to steal. This can be done at the doctor's office or at home. What also helps is poor hygiene. That'll make you gross and of "poor quality." I don't recommend this practice, but if you're absolutely certain that a Tridentum is lurking in the streets, it's best not to shower for a few days.

How to Attract This Creature:
Good health and top fitness make a Tridentum see you as an excellent candidate to take "accessories" from.

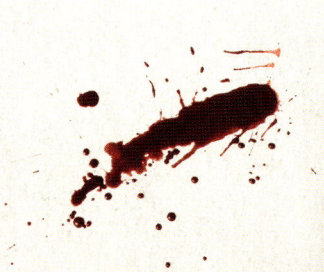

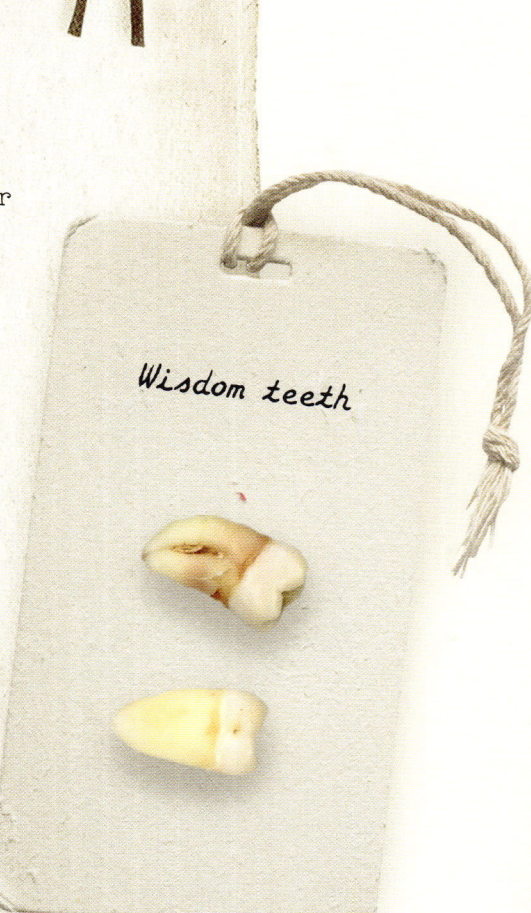

Wisdom teeth

TRIDENTUM

Tridenta are trendsetters. If a Tridentum trend catches on, it won't be long before other creatures want to join in. Unfortunately, not all creatures are as careful and precise as Tridenta. In Belgium, for example, a troll once saw a Tridentum wearing a beautiful necklace made from human wisdom teeth. The troll wanted to recreate that iconic look, but it killed eleven people in the process. A similar incident occurred in Germany when goblins discovered that appendix scarves were the new Tridentum trend. Forty people died and were found without an appendix.

Fortunately, governments keep a close eye on Tridentum trends and try to make it as difficult as possible for these creatures to collect accessories. Occasionally, they want to prevent a dangerous trend from taking over. They do that by removing certain human body parts before Tridenta have a chance to do so.

Some individuals seem to have been born without wisdom teeth, but we cannot rule out the possibility that they may have been visited by a Tridentum during their childhood. My sister is one of those people. Did she really never have wisdom teeth? Or did a Tridentum take them?

Tridenta are very careful when they remove certain parts from a human body. In fact, they're so careful that you probably won't even notice that they've paid you a visit. They always make sure that you're not harmed. If you know someone who's missing certain body parts and has no explanation for it, it may be the work of a Tridentum.

This Tridentum's clothing is made of the rarest spider web and the most expensive freshwater pearls you can find. Human wisdom teeth make the elegant outfit edgy and dazzling.

These posh creatures don't sell their exclusive accessories to anyone. If you want to look like a Tridentum, you must recreate its look yourself.

Personal Encounter:

When I was fifteen years old, I went to a flea market in Spain and bought a compass from a merchant. When I was about to put it in my pocket, an elderly woman approached me. She warned me not to use the compass on my travels. Her late husband was lost at sea because of a similar compass. The last message she had received from him was a telegram. All our compasses have stopped working for no reason STOP. We're lost at sea STOP. Storm is coming STOP. Our boat is sinking STOP. Something is nibbling on my iron-toed boots STOP. After that, she never heard from him again. She believes that little men called Minarorbises were responsible for her husband's disappearance.

Species:
Iron ore creature

Habitat:
Minarorbises live in large underwater communities just below the sandy bottom. They're found in so-called dead zones: areas where compasses don't work. A good example of this is the Bermuda Triangle. Dead zones are thought to be caused by a mineral in the soil. This is partly true, but the rare metal is actually in the Minarorbises. Their heads and arms are made of it. In addition, their bellies are filled with iron ore. With their large population and metal-rich bodies, they create a magnetic field, which causes compasses to malfunction.

Size:
About the size of a seagull

Food:
Iron ore and other metals. Because Minarorbises can create magnetic fields, they can also alter the navigation of ships and planes. They spin in circles until their fuel depletes. Then the Minarorbises puncture their metal exterior, causing them to sink to the ocean floor. What remains is a feast for Minarorbises.

How to Protect Yourself:
Even though Minarorbises don't consume meat, they're still extremely dangerous to humans. If your compass starts spinning, there's a good chance you're in Minarorbis territory. To be sure of this, you can take a powerful magnet, attach it to a fishing rod, and lower it into the water. If you catch one with your magnet, stop using your compass immediately. You'll have to use alternative means of navigation, such as the stars and the sun. I highly recommend traveling on a wooden vessel, as opposed to a metal one.

Compass {

MINARORBIS

Many people believe that most supernatural creatures are allergic to metal, but this isn't true. In fact, Minarorbises are made of one of the most pure and dense types of metal in the world.

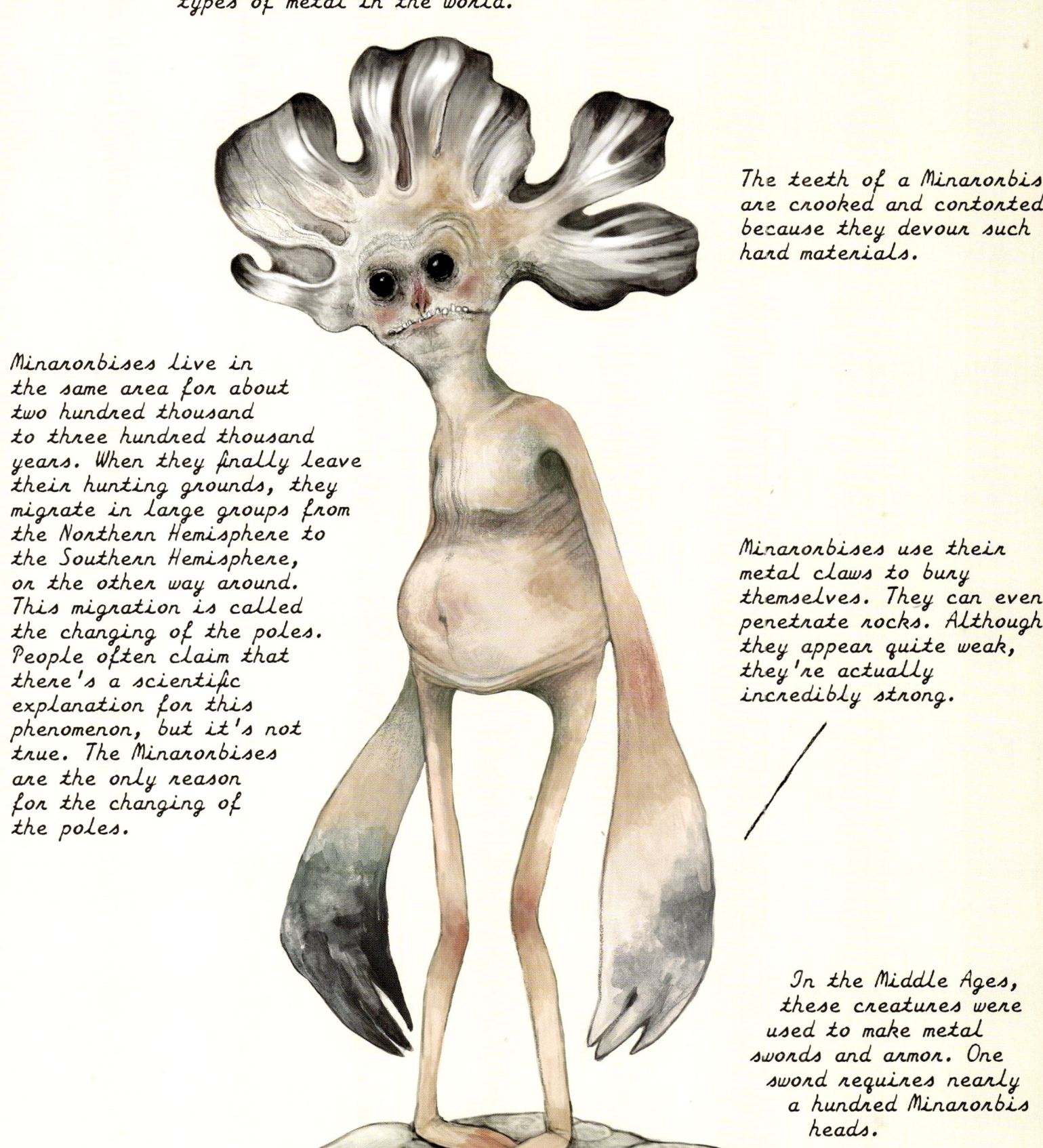

The teeth of a Minarorbis are crooked and contorted because they devour such hard materials.

Minarorbises live in the same area for about two hundred thousand to three hundred thousand years. When they finally leave their hunting grounds, they migrate in large groups from the Northern Hemisphere to the Southern Hemisphere, or the other way around. This migration is called the changing of the poles. People often claim that there's a scientific explanation for this phenomenon, but it's not true. The Minarorbises are the only reason for the changing of the poles.

Minarorbises use their metal claws to bury themselves. They can even penetrate rocks. Although they appear quite weak, they're actually incredibly strong.

In the Middle Ages, these creatures were used to make metal swords and armor. One sword requires nearly a hundred Minarorbis heads.

Personal Encounter:

I bought this strange stone in a small gift shop near a windy cave in a seaside village in France. It's from a Windfish, a strange walking fish species that lives in windy caves near bodies of water. To avoid being blown away every time it goes ashore to look for food, it has developed stones in its body. Those stones are very precious and rare, and they're often used to make jewelry. For that reason, many Windfish are captured and killed. I didn't discover that horrible fact until years later. I haven't worn my necklace with the Windfish stone ever since.

Species:
Fish

Habitat:
Windy caves
near water

Size:
About the size of a fat rat

Food:
Only soft foods, such as algae, snails, and even tasty mud

How to Protect Yourself:
Windfish themselves aren't dangerous at all, but there's a strange phenomenon called wind insanity. Windfish are accustomed to constant strong winds. If the wind suddenly stops in their cave, they become insane. They still aren't particularly dangerous, but they may try to bite you. So, my advice is to stay away from caves near water on windless days.

How to Attract This Creature:
If you want to lure these creatures, you need to find a very powerful fan and go to a windy cave. Turn the fan on there and wait. If everything goes according to plan, the Windfish will come to the fan. But please don't abuse that trick, as they're an endangered species.

Reproduction:
Female and male Windfish have the same way of attracting mates: growing their stones. The larger the stones, the easier the egg-laying will be. The female can then sit down in peace while the male sits in front of her to make sure the eggs aren't blown away. After the eggs hatch, the baby Windfish are immediately blown into the water. They eat whatever they find there. When the food runs out, their main objective is to return to their parents. They have to develop their own stones to go ashore. Some Windfish fail to do so and are blown back into the water. They then become food for the new batch of babies. Yes, these fish are cannibals, but frighteningly, only when they're babies.

Windfish stone

WINDFISH

These creatures love large stones, but some Windfishes' stones become so large that they can no longer move. That's extremely dangerous because they could starve, and they cannot flee when poachers and stone collectors enter their caves.

If you want to keep one as a pet – which I don't recommend – make sure you have an aquarium with a water part and a land part. Place a small but powerful fan on the land section and always provide it with enough power. After all, if these fish are without wind for a day, they'll go completely bonkers.

The stones in their bodies aren't only pretty, but they also help cure certain ailments. If you get carsick or seasick, a drink with ground Windfish stones will cure you.

Windfish originally lived underwater in windy caves, but they had to go ashore because there wasn't enough food. The problem was that their weak bodies couldn't stand up to the strong winds. After years of evolution, they finally found a way not to be blown away every time they left the water: developing stones to weigh down their bodies.

Baby Windfish have very sharp teeth. However, they lose these as they get older. That's because their body then focuses entirely on the production of stones, so it'll no longer produce any other hard materials.

Personal Encounter:

I found this creature in shallow water. Her shell was full of holes and filled with seaweed. Since she looked awfully sad, I decided to find a better shell for this little lady and propose a trade: her shell for mine. When I added some fish sticks, she gladly accepted my offer. She now has a stronger and better home and I have a cool shell with holes.

Species:
Snail

Subspecies:
Sea snail

Habitat:
The North Sea

Size:
Typically the size of a large sea snail, but can grow to the size of a human

Food:
Small crabs, jellyfish, and fried fish (especially fish sticks)

How to Protect Yourself:
While these snail princesses are usually harmless to humans, they'll bite if you step on them. Fortunately, their bite isn't poisonous. The question with these creatures isn't how to protect yourself, but rather how to protect them. If children play with them by the sea, ensure they're safely returned.

Transformation:
When an ordinary sea snail turns 25, she transforms into a snail princess. Snails are often seen as pests, but if you're patient and respect these wondrous creatures, they can turn into beautiful ladies. This is also the case with snails that live on the land. Unfortunately, many people harm snails out of fear. My twin brother is one of these people.

Shell

SNAIL PRINCESS

Most of these ladies are fairly small, but occasionally one grows to be as large as a human. During this process, she grows legs and abandons her shell to walk on land. She can choose to become a human or live as a crazy sea witch. I personally prefer the latter.

Many believe that snail princesses have no souls and that they can only earn one by marrying a man. This is nonsense. Men drafted this scheme in hopes of marrying the snail princesses.

This snail princess has only one arm. She lost her other arm when children caught her in their net. One of the children said that her arm would regrow. When it didn't, they threw her back in the net. Over time, her arm has grown stronger, and she's actively plotting her revenge.

Because they have gills, snail princesses can breathe underwater and above water.

Personal Encounter:

When my father, who is a professional diver, was exploring the shipwreck of the Red Sea Dragon in Egypt, he discovered a seemingly horrendous creature called the Nymhalum. My father said that there was only one other living creature on the wreck: a moray named Molly. Apparently, the Nymhalum considers Molly her only friend. My father found one of the creature's scales on the sea floor and gave it to me. Taking things from the sea is typically forbidden, but this was worth it.

Mermaid scale

Species:
Mermaid

Subspecies:
Cave mermaid. Cave mermaids appear frightening due to their missing eyes, but they're actually quite similar to other mermaids.

Habitat:
The wreck of the Red Sea Dragon in the Red Sea near Egypt. The Nymhalum was born and raised in the saltwater caves of the Red Sea. One day, she ventured outside her caves and never found her way back . . .

Size:
The size of a human

Food:
She devours nearly everything she sees: fish, insects, birds . . . Fortunately, she usually doesn't attack people—unless provoked. The locals believe it's because she views humans as an extension of her own family.

How to Protect Yourself:
Let Molly be! The Nymhalum is lonely; she needs her friend. Taking or harming Molly could lead to disaster.

NYMHALUM

The Nymhalum was born in saltwater caves. In those caves, there was no light. That's why she's an albino and has no eyes.

The Nymhalum uses the red leaves around her head to hunt. She senses the vibrations in the water and attacks. She's an effective and merciless huntress. When given the opportunity, she even eats sharks.

This creature is allergic to sunlight and hides during the day. At night, she swims around the wreck with Molly.

The Nymhalum shares her dreams, hopes, and struggles with Molly. Molly is a very good listener.

At the wreck of the Red Sea Dragon, there are no fish, crabs, jellyfish, or shellfish. Anything edible is eaten by the Nymhalum. The only exceptions are humans and Molly.

Fishing near the wreck of the Red Sea Dragon is illegal. If you accidentally kill Molly, this mermaid will retaliate.

Personal Encounter:

When I was eleven years old, I went diving with my family in Egypt. While I was waiting on the land in between dives, a young Bedouin, one of the local nomads, approached me. She gave me a small doll made of beads and told me a peculiar story about a Sea Goblin named One Eared Larry. Male Sea Goblins are born blind, but have incredible hearing. And female Sea Goblins are born deaf, but have amazing eyesight. Females like to mate with the male with the biggest ears, and males like to mate with the female with the biggest eyes. But One Eared Larry was born with only one ear. Because of that, no female Sea Goblin wanted to mate with him. The poor wretch felt deeply unhappy. One day, Larry was crying in a puddle on the beach when the Bedouin found him. She felt bad for him and gave him a piece of handmade jewelry: a little lady made of beads with a bell under her skirt, just like the little doll she gave to me. Larry was instantly in love. It was love at first sound. Thanks to his bell bride, Larry could hear better; he could even pick up ultrasonic sounds. This allowed him to spot predators from a very long distance. Other Sea Goblins started to notice that Larry was hidden before they ever saw or heard a predator. This made him very popular with the ladies. But Larry remained loyal to his bell woman. He was happily married and planned on keeping it that way!

Species:
Goblin

Subspecies:
Sea Goblin

Habitat:
The Red Sea off Egypt. Sea Goblins live in shallow water on the sandy bottom. They can also occasionally be found at sunset on land at low tide. Direct sunlight is very bad for their skin.

Size:
About the size of a tall glass of water

Food:
Sea Goblins use their crab-like claws to scrape algae off rocks, and the tentacles on their heads to catch plankton and small sea creatures.
They can retract their tentacles into their heads to "eat" them clean.

Relationship to Humans:
Sea Goblins are friendly and harmless, but they're wary of humans. Because of their bright blue color, they're often hunted for jewelry. The only humans they have contact with are small children. At low tide, Sea Goblins can be seen playing in sea foam and puddles, where young children often look for shells. Sea Goblins like to find shells to give to children.

Stonefish?

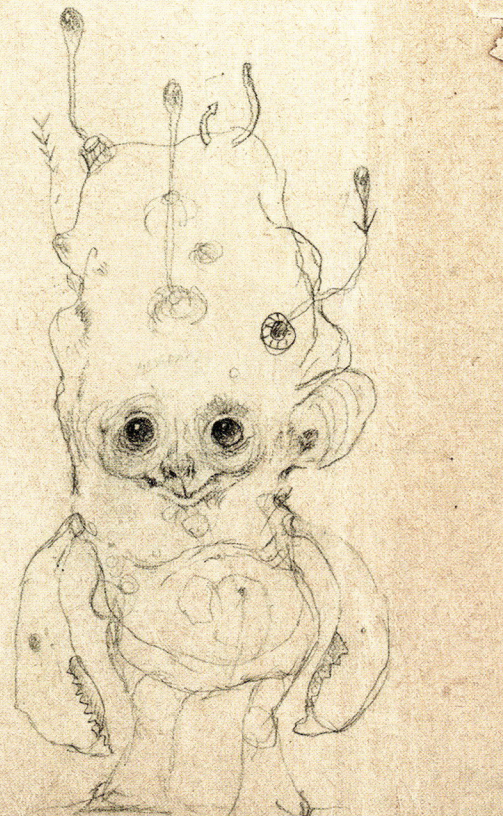

ONE EARED LARRY

Sea Goblins are extremely easy to kill. Their soft belly and head make them easy targets for predators. They can't really fight back, but they're incredibly good at hiding. With their large claws, these creatures can dig holes for themselves at lightning speed, and because their head and belly are so squishy, they're able to fit themselves in the smallest of places.

Sea Goblins choose their own names—unusual names like Moon Slayer, The Blue Menace, and Danger.

The greatest enemy of these creatures is the Stonefish. It has happened more than once that a Sea Goblin tried to hide in a hole in a rock, which turned out to be the open mouth of a Stonefish.

These creatures are made up of 88 percent water.

Some Sea Goblins once tried to wage war against a Stonefish. But after three weeks of "battle", it turned out that the Stonefish was actually just a stone. The battle was called the Great War with the Deceptive Stonefish. There were no casualties.

Doll

The texture of their skin is best described as a mixture between that of a jellyfish and a lobster.

Sea Goblins can jump, but not very high.

1

Junatin wing

When I was on a vacation in Egypt, a curious Junatin decided to snoop around in my luggage. I only discovered that she had traveled with me when I opened my suitcase in the Netherlands. The Junatin wasn't happy at all about her unplanned move. She terrorized my house for the first few days by sewing or unstitching everything I owned. The sleeves of my blouses were stitched together, and all of my dresses fell off their hangers. One time, she had even sewn my pajamas into the mattress while I was sleeping! After that incident, I did some research. I read that I should leave needles and honey around my house. Fortunately, this worked. After two weeks, the Junatin finally came around and even offered me a peace offering: one of her wings. I now only drink very sweet tea and always have a cup ready for my little friend. In addition, I scatter needles in random places around my house. My boyfriend isn't very happy about that because he has pricked himself many times.

Species:
Elf

Habitat:
Deserts. They avoid human encounters. They require minimal water to survive.

Size:
About the size of a praying mantis

Food:
Sugar, honey, and sweet tea

How to Protect Yourself:
Junatins can be two things: a good friend or a fearsome enemy. If you leave a sugary cup of tea or a small cup of honey, they'll help you with things that need sewing. But if you somehow manage to betray them, your life will be miserable. Your pants will be sewn shut, your shirts will be too small, and your house will be a nightmare.

Reproduction:
Since the male Junatins don't have wings, they usually stay home to care for the children. Junatins are very kind to each other and have a stable and happy life. They have a special relationship with their partner and usually mate for life. Their community is positive and accepting. We should all be a little more like the Junatins.

JUNATIN

Junatins are born with three wings on their heads. These wings have no practical use, but they're used as gifts. They're given to people they value.

A person who befriends multiple Junatins could start a successful clothing business, pending the Junatins are treated with respect and kindness. This is ideal for small local businesses.

These creatures are obsessed with needles. They even hold contests to determine who has the best needle.

Junatins use their six hands to sew very quickly. They sew about 23 times faster than humans.

Although they're very friendly to their own kind, Junatins are extremely unfriendly to humans. If you don't have access to sweet tea or honey, it's advised that you avoid Junatins altogether.

If you anger this species, your mouth, ears, and eyes can be sewn shut. This isn't deadly, but it's very traumatizing. Junatins usually only do this if you've killed one of them. It doesn't matter if it was intentional or accidental. So, make sure you never kill a Junatin.

At night, Egyptians often set out a small glass of honey beside articles of clothing in need of mending. When they wake, the honey is gone and the clothes are repaired. Because Junatins have an insatiable passion for sewing, they'll mend anything you give them. But this must be done in moderation. Otherwise, things can quickly get out of hand.

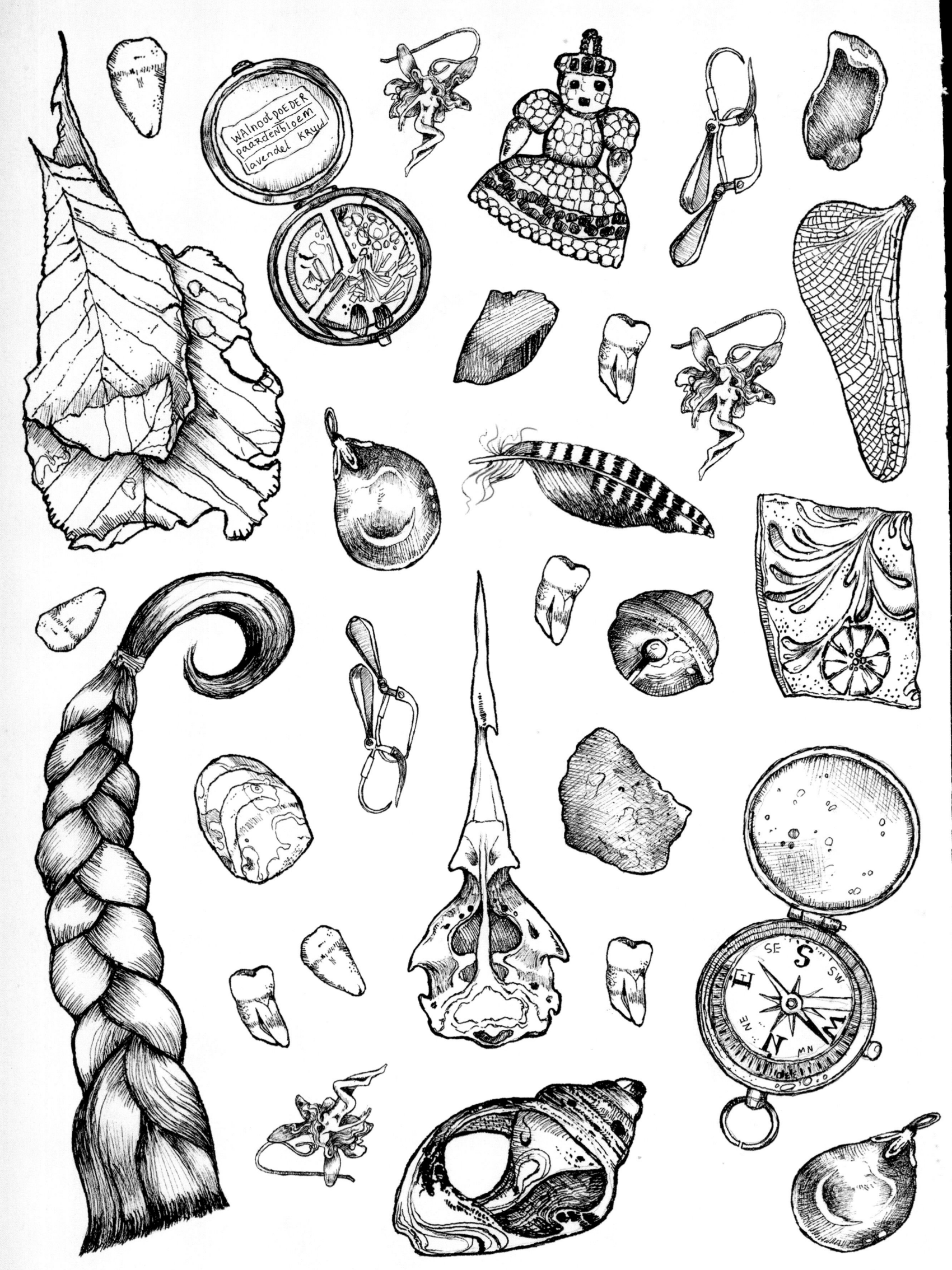